I SPY

LIGHTNING IN THE SKY

For Allen
and his cousin Dave
—J.M.

For Maya Griffin
—W.W.

Text copyright © 2005 by Jean Marzollo.
Illustrations copyright © 1999 by Walter Wick.

All rights reserved. Published by Scholastic Inc.
SCHOLASTIC, CARTWHEEL BOOKS, and associated logos
are trademarks and/or registered trademarks of Scholastic Inc.
Lexile is a registered trademark of MetaMetrics, Inc.

All images by Walter Wick taken from *I Spy Treasure Hunt*.
Published by Scholastic Inc. in 1999.

Library of Congress Cataloging-in-Publication Data is available.

ISBN-13: 978-0-439-68052-3
ISBN-10: 0-439-68052-2

30 29 28 27 26 25 24   40   12 13 14/0

Printed in the U.S.A. 40 • This edition first printing, August 2008

I SPY
LIGHTNING IN THE SKY

Riddles by Jean Marzollo
Photographs by Walter Wick

Cartwheel
·B·O·O·K·S· ®

SCHOLASTIC INC.
New York   Toronto   London   Auckland   Sydney
Mexico City   New Delhi   Hong Kong   Buenos Aires

I spy

 a truck,

a lighthouse light,

a jack,

and a lightning bolt
at night.

I spy

a tiny toy
cannon,

 a 3,

a brown starfish,

 and two shells
from the sea.

I spy

a stop sign,

a wet blue duck,

Sharky's shack,

and a yellow truck.

I spy

a shell,

two oars,

 LOST CAT,

a fish,

and a biker in a red hat.

I spy

a screw,

 a pair of wings,

a key in a jar,

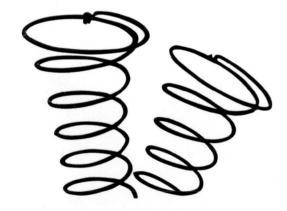

and two large springs.

I spy

a ladder,

a boat on a trailer,

 ONE WAY,

and a statue of a sailor.

I spy

a starfish,

a seagull,

a seal,

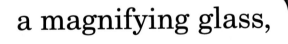 a magnifying glass,

and a silver
ship's wheel.

I spy

an arrow,

a pail on a string,

a furry groundhog,

and a tire swing.

I spy

an oar,

 a ship,

a plane,

 TOW-AWAY ZONE,

and a rusty chain.

I spy

 a trash can,

a red suitcase,

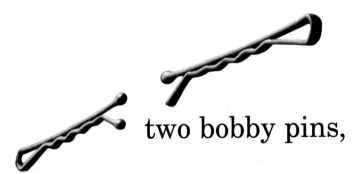 two bobby pins,

and a president's face.

I spy two matching words.

tiny toy cannon

two large springs

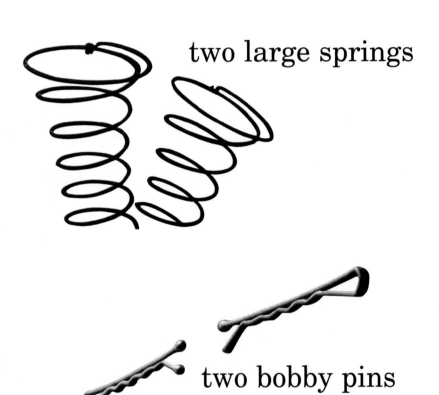

two bobby pins

I spy two matching words.

statue of a sailor

 pair of wings

trash can

I spy two words that start with the letter S.

 seal

 suitcase

 groundhog

I spy two words that start with the letter L.

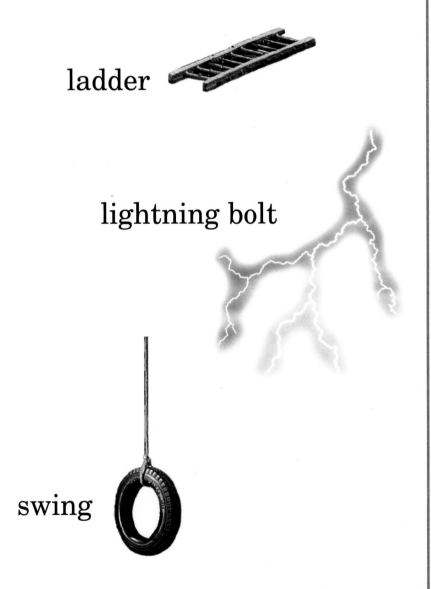

ladder

lightning bolt

swing

I spy two words that end with the letters LL.

seagull

shell

wheel

I spy two words that end with the letters NG.

pail on a string

tire swing

statue

I spy two words that rhyme.

plane

oars

rusty chain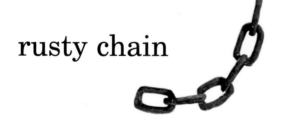

I spy two words that rhyme.

 fish

trailer

sailor